BRONZE-WINGED
BUTTERFLY

BRONZE-WINGED
BUTTERFLY

LUKE R. GREGERSON

ARCHWAY
PUBLISHING

Archway Publishing books may be ordered through booksellers or by contacting:

Archway Publishing
1663 Liberty Drive
Bloomington, IN 47403
www.archwaypublishing.com
844-669-3957

ISBN: 978-1-6657-1474-7 (sc)
ISBN: 978-1-6657-1475-4 (e)

Library of Congress Control Number: 2021922298

Print information available on the last page.

Archway Publishing rev. date: 01/05/2022

TO MOM AND DAD
SORRY I COULDN'T FINISH THIS SOON
FOR YOU TO READ DAD

PART ONE

THE MAKING OF...

CHAPTER ONE

I rolled up a tortilla stuffed with peanut butter and dog-boned it in my mouth, then picked up my notebook, pen, and glass of ice water. I wedged my elbow behind the handle on the sliding glass door and shifted it open with my funny bone, just enough to slip through onto my apartment balcony. The view was always gorgeous from the seventh floor, even though it was a bit of a monotone gray. The bit of green in the distance always got to me.

That early, the sun was behind my apartment, filling my single room with a bright orange, lighting the concrete horizon at such an angle to send shadows sideways. I placed my water, notebook, and pen on my round glass table which sat between a set of padded rocking chairs that looked recently dried out from the rain a day prior. I turned my breakfast 90 degrees° and took a bite as I sat down. I sighed through and tongued out some peanut butter from an old wisdom tooth divot.

I sipped some water and looked at balconies on either side of me. The one on my direct left was decorated with many potted plants, some newly transplanted and others showing signs of overwatering. The balcony after had two large poles with a drying line running between them, airing out a large tan comforter, even though our units were furnished with dryers. I wasn't sure whose it was, as I had recently noticed a young couple packing up and moving out from that unit. The two balconies to the right of me were about as notable as my own. I never saw much of a point in decorating a temporary space. I always seemed to bounce from place to place, to whatever jobs could cover my bills.

My parents liked to toss around the term "starving artist," but it never really felt like a fit to me. I worked where I could find it and, in a literal sense, my meals were fine; I just often wasn't that hungry. I suppose any artist could be "starving" if they just didn't want to eat. In between this or that odd job, I spent most of my spare time watching videos on my phone or messing around on my computer, but I also submitted my own short stories and poetry to various publishers. My work was occasionally accepted by free publications, and payment came in what little reputation that local journals would accrue to me. It's hard to write without expecting fame or fortune. Luckily, I have always been comfortable living by my means; money has never been the biggest motivator for me.

I glanced out over Omaha, a city I grew up in, left for years, and found my way back to. The city and buildings seemed to grow alongside me. Streets like veins, cars like blood, and all those organs flicking on their lights to start another day of keeping the city functioning. Just outside the city the land is flat-very flat.

One thing I always loved about Omaha was that in a half hour you could find yourself on farmland. I grew up passing the corn that was "knee high by fourth of July" on the drives to school with mom. Us neighborhood kids would run around the undeveloped plots of houses with shovels and dig for fun until our blisters had splinters. And the city grew. It shaved off the fields of wheat like early peach fuzz. Grew tall buildings like adolescent muscles. Connecting roads and bridges to other cities like early flings of love.

Looking out at the small downtown always made me miss the green tree lines and quickly budding crops in fields. I would often think about how I would trade the pigeons that fly by for the robins that had nested outside my childhood bedroom window. I flipped open my notebook and glanced through all my near-illegible scrawl. Calls to action to make Wordsworth squirm. I would always worry about being heavy handed. I looked over the previous page.

SWEAT AND WATER

The heat bears down on you,
as you like it to do
while in our garden pruning stray stems.
I love to watch and hear your quiet giggles
about the aesthetic choices I suggest.
For fun I tell you to lop off whatever flower
looks the best.
It's been an hour.
After doing my own,
I apply more sunscreen to the back of your
neck, already pink.
Bending over you with a towel,
I dab your sweat
and count how many flowers you have left.
Just a small row.
Still bent, I pick up your water bottle
and sprinkle it onto the artificial flowers.
You giggle again.

I never submitted it.

"Morning, Lynn," came from my left. My neighbor, Marine, stepped out onto her balcony in her holey bathrobe, carrying a small watering can. She was older, hair mostly gray and skin suntanned with wrinkles, but her smile was always warm. The robe seemed to hang in just the right spots to conceal the parts of her body that I silently hoped would remain concealed. As long as she was comfortable, I supposed.

"Good morning. How are you?" I asked while she began to sprinkle the pots. So much so in fact, that even from a distance I could see the water stream from the draining holes and darken the wood of the deck.

"Oh, just fine, dear," she replied, her soft voice hardly carrying to my balcony. She went back inside to fill up the watering can as she talked. "It's a lovely morning," her voice piped up from inside. "Monte went out to grab some bagels and juice and a newspaper. I'll toss one over to you when he gets back," she said, her voice growing louder until she appeared again.

"Don't worry about it; got my breakfast here." I shook the nub of taco shell. "Thanks, though."

"Working on some poems already? This early?" she asked.

"Trying to."

"Not going very well?"

"Not really."

"Oooh! You could do another one about love and the blooming lilies! I still have that little poem from the paper hanging on my fridge," she said excitedly. I glanced at what I had been writing, a flashback to innocent love that could sometimes help inspire me.

"No particular muses at the moment," I replied politely. I decided not to mention the fact that making the same poem over again seemed a bit pointless.

"A shame; you know how I adore your nature imagery, even if it can be a bit doom and gloom at times."

"Yeah."

"Are you writing about the stuff in the news? The ice caps shifting and pollution and whatnot?" her volume fading, refilling again.

"Ehh, a bit," I spoke up so she could hear.

"Well it's good to see someone try and make a difference, even if it is just with their words."

"Yeah."

I clicked my pen a few times. Marine meant all the best by this - that words are difficult tools to make an impact with - and I knew that. Still, advocating and practicing change were a bit of a disconnect for me. I was never one to attend a rally or march. Not that I didn't care about the movements; I just hated being in a mob of people for hours. I'd cleaned yards or public areas a few times, but it was always for some sort of pay. I recycled. I also read that collecting and processing recycling costs more energy than it could ever make up for, unless the country puts in policy to support it. So if my beer cans ever started to overflow, sometimes they ended up with the food scraps, and I didn't lose a bit of sleep about it.

But being in nature, then seeing the city compared to forests or lakes always made me write. Even if I couldn't get my ass away from whatever show I was watching, seeing the world online could take me anywhere, and writing about it was something I had always been comfortable with. If writing about how nature was being ruined could keep my favorite campgrounds around a few more years, then I'd use all my selfishness for the good of the planet.

"Just nothing with any cursing again, or the sex. I just can't bring myself to share it with anyone that way," she said, draining the can again.

"Nature is full of sex though," I pointed out with a slight raise of my brow.

"I guess so... I like the cute ones more."

"Thanks, I'll keep that in mind," I replied, unsure what else to say.

"No work then today?"

"Not today; got Saturdays off now. Not much going on, so I thought I'd stay out here a bit."

"Sounds lovely. Take care, dear."

"You too," I said as Marine smiled at me, turned her back, and returned inside, robe revealing pale skin that may have never seen the sunlight. I breathed shallowly. I turned a page and stared at it. It was a mild day, bit of a breeze but it would probably warm up once the sun was overhead. As I looked back out over the city, the early rush-hour traffic made the streets look like a blood clot. I looked at the tall, downtown buildings, so out of place. As if a single square block of New York grew right in the center of Omaha. I looked at the glinting windows, so bright with orange. Blinding bright. So bright it made my brain catch fire. My eyes fluttered. I blacked out.

CHAPTER TWO

I woke up with light behind my eyes and tears running down my cheeks. Squinting my eyes as hard as possible still let in the red heat of the sun through my eyelids.

The pain started to dull as quickly as it came. I realized my mouth was clenched so tight that my jaw muscles were struggling to relax. My mouth was dry, either from what had just happened or the peanut butter. I cracked my eyes open; they beat out of tenderness. A few tears trailed to my cheeks and shirt.

It didn't seem much later in the day; the sun wasn't overhead. I dug my phone from my pocket and, through half-sealed eyes, saw that I had only lost about a half hour. I assumed anyway. The city streets were flowing more normally, but still at a slow pace. The glint off the cityscape was much calmer, but it left stings on my sensitive eyes. My nervous hand weakly and cautiously brought my glass of water to my lips. The remaining bits of ice helped cool and relax me. My breathing eased. I looked down at the blank page in my lap.

Write this down, a thought appeared in my head. It wasn't my thought, but I had it. It was like any other thought, in the usual type of internal voice, I simply didn't make it. As if someone else was playing my brain like an instrument.

"The fuck..." I stammered out. I looked around for someone to answer. Aside from this stray thought, nothing was out of the ordinary. I lived alone, and no one appeared to be on any other balcony. Peering inside, I saw nothing. I rose to my feet. Attempting to ease myself over the railing a bit to gaze into the balconies above and below me proved both difficult and fruitless. Had someone been on another balcony speaking, it wouldn't have made sense how the voice came so clearly into my mind.

"H-hello?" stammered from my lips. Shaking, I lowered myself back into my chair. My mind was blank for a moment. I took another sip of water, iceless at this point. There was probably an easy explanation. I had just passed out, I must have just been sick. I wasn't sure since I had only ever passed out from drinking too much. Maybe I cracked the back of my head against the chair when I sat down. I thought about calling over to a neighbor when my train of thought interrupted itself again.

Please, write what I say and your responses down. Including the last few moments. I will be able to explain what is happening, but you must notate our conversation, I thought unwillingly. Hesitant, but unsure of what other options I had, I readied my pen and notebook and wrote what had been said; the greeting, my response, a pause, my hello, another pause, and, as accurately as I could remember, what my brain had just said to itself. These unknown thoughts I marked with a ? -, and my own as a simple L -. I thought my notation looked fairly accurate to what happened.

Also include the current date, time, and your location at the top of the page. I tapped on my phone that was resting on the glass table to see the time and date, which, considering the circumstances, slipped my mind. I squinted hard as the light bounced from its screen and into my tearful eyes.

8

"Okay," I said to space. I fidgeted nervously, hunched over the notebook, leg jittering, waiting. After sitting anxiously for as long as I could stand, I asked out loud, "Who are you? What's happening?" writing as I spoke.

After a moment I got a reply in my head. I copied down what I thought quickly.

I know this might feel odd, but it is completely safe. It is a pleasure to message you. This sort of communication has rarely been used outside of trials. I hope it is as painless and simple as the scientists have told me it is. They ask that I let you know that you falling unconscious is a natural part of this, so do not worry about long term brain damage.

I was at a loss. My hand worked on autopilot as I tried to get a hold of the situation, but it was difficult. While I was thinking this longer message, I was unable to think on my own, as my brain was already being used for thinking. It didn't feel like something I could fight off or stop. Since my mind was already occupied, it was difficult to grasp exactly what I was telling myself. Once the intrusive thoughts would pause at a sentence, I would process it quickly before it went to the next, as if what I had thought snapped into clarity. Once I could understand what I was forced to think I would jot it down. Hearing my own thoughts tell me not to worry about losing control was more worrying than comforting.

What I will tell you may seem impossible, but realize I am already communicating with you through your thoughts. You are a writer in your time. You are to write about the future, as it has already happened, and I am supposed to describe the world to you that your generation, and the following two, have left behind. It paused for a longer moment. I caught up in my notation.

"How would I do that? And who are you?" I asked again.

I'm your great-great-grandson and, sadly, I'll never get a chance to meet you. Even now, this is a bit of a one-sided conversation. I'm currently in the future and I am to share the information that will help you call the public to action about the world. This made even less sense to me. It was an easier fact to accept that I had lost my mind.

"And how would I help the world?" I said a bit quieter as I wrote, not sure where my questions were being heard from.

As you well know, the Earth's environment is deteriorating in your time. If I describe the future to you and you write poems about them, they will be able to spur on others to help bring the world to a sustainable position. It will take years and years for the more hard-headed people to understand what is going on, but as the newer generations come, the more opportunities you will have to sway opinions.

While the answers I got were very clear, they were so unexpected that they didn't make sense at the moment. I sat, rereading my own messy, shaky handwriting. I was left alone with my self-controlled thoughts for a moment as I turned my page. Things like the environment being in danger made sense to me, but someone talking to me from the future, a long-distance-by-time relative, seemed impossible, and I had to question how this was happening.

I had never passed out like that before and I wondered if I was sick. My brain and the space behind my eyes had stopped hurting. The only thing I felt was sweaty and a bit nauseous. Both could have been pinned on my nerves at the time. Everything had happened so quickly and out of my control, yet my own thoughts were telling me to be calm and to try and to listen to these strange, new suggestions.

"How is this working then? How could my great-great-grandson from the future contact me? I don't even have a kid," I said quieter still. I was beginning to feel that it didn't matter how loud I spoke.

In due time. You won't believe me if I tell you yet. I have to make you believe that I am telling the truth and not just a symptom of an illness.

My thoughts tried to reason with me, but I had so many questions that I decided to move on to the next topic at hand.

"If I'm supposed to write about the environment of the future to try and save it, then the future must be some kinda wasteland," I said. Maybe the worst would eventually come. The world could one day become an uninhabitable urban hell where clean air is a commodity. Kids would daydream about leaving their bunkers.

No, not a wasteland, just different. Not what someone of your time would expect if they had been planning for the worst. To that I was confused, bending my brow at the page as I wrote the opposite answer of what I had expected.

"Well, then…What is it like?"

It may take some time to tell you every detail, but just know the world is safe. The poetry and stories that you and others will write will help people come to the realization that corrections were needed to be taken to help keep the Earth habitable. Discussing the future health of the world will be a regular occurrence. If you listen to what I tell you, and you already have since I am in the result of your work. The ways of daily life will change to help undo the damages that had been done to the environment.

I was hesitant to believe anything I was thinking, but my mind had never gone off on its own before. Not in this way anyway. It felt too real to not be true. I suppose I will never know if it is, as I will never be able to meet my great-great-grandson or see the world when and where he grows up.

Let me show you some of the countryside from my time. Write some notes down after seeing it. It will help give you an idea of what the world to come is like. I should let you know that the scientists say that it helps to close your eyes. I started to catch faint visions in my head, yet it was a bit fuzzy, muddled by the notes occupying most of my forethought. After adding a final period after "eyes" I took a breath and slowly shut them.

My senses were taken over and I was thinking back to a memory of a place I had never been to. The image in my head was so real, but unlike anything I had ever seen or could imagine. My eyes opened again, and I began writing down a description of what I saw. I couldn't write fast enough. Hundreds of words all stuck at the tip of my pen, patiently waiting their turns to get onto the page.

What I wrote was left in my notes for quite a while. It took me a good year before I could describe what I saw in that flash with any sort of articulation. My great-great-grandson told me a few more details after my daydream. He helped me clear up the sounds I heard, the smell of the air, and told me about the structures I saw. This is what I would write a year later:

DIRTY TO STALE

THE AIR IS ALWAYS STALE.
PURE, BUT STALE.
CLOUDS OF SMOG AND CARBON
FILTERED THROUGH
TALL, STEEL TOWERS ON THE MOUNTAIN RIDGE.
MASSIVE TUNNELS ON UPSIDE-DOWN V-SHAPED
LEGS,
FILTHY ON ONE SIDE FROM THE THICK AIR,
LIKE A BLACK MOSS ON A METAL TRUNK.

THERE ARE A FEW OTHER TRUNKS SCATTERED
AROUND.
A ONCE THICK FOREST TRADED FOR A GREY-BROWN
ROCK FACE.
LASERS REMOVE THE C OF CO_2.
I'VE HEARD THAT YOU CAN HEAR THE POPPING
WHEN THEY WORK OVERTIME.
IT'S EFFICIENT,
"SAVES SPACE," THEY TELL US,
"THEY MAKE PLENTY OF AIR."

CHAPTER THREE

Now, *I'll have to pause for about fifteen minutes.*
"Why is that?" I asked myself. The next moment I heard a familiar nails-on-a-chalkboard squeak from two balconies to my left. My surprise shook me away from my paper I had been staring at intently, now dry-eyed. I unfurled my cramped grip on the pen after jotting down "15-minute break" and realized the paper was wavy with sweat from my hand. I flipped my book closed out of instinct, not that anyone would question me having it opened. It wasn't out of the ordinary for me to sit out on my balcony to write. If anything was out of the ordinary, it was that I was writing so intently, instead of my usual mindless pen clicking as I waited for something to happen.

The large, tan comforter on the far balcony waved as the apartment's landlord stepped out. I moved in a few months ago and had hardly interacted with him, so I was surprised when he remembered my name. I, however, had forgotten his the moment his business card went into my pocket when we started discussing my move.

"Oh! Hello Lynn! How's the place?" He looked the same as I remembered; taller, middle-aged, thinning brown hair. He was a bit heavy and currently sweating through what I think was the same red polo shirt tucked into khaki pants as the day I signed my lease. When he asked me the question, a friendly smile flickered on his lips, but fell due to deep breaths of fatigue.

"Pretty good, no complaints," I replied, pressing my notebook to my lap, hoping to hide it even more, "How's it goin'?"

"Not too bad, just cleaning up the place since the unit is empty now. Gettin' it ready to show," he said tugging at the center of his shirt repeatedly to circulate out the sweaty air. He paused for a moment and silence lingered in the air a bit longer than comfortable. "I guess the guy had been sleeping on the couch for a while, there was a lot of bedding on it. They washed it before leaving but just left it on the couch, wet, so it just reeks of mildew in here now."

"Huh, I never heard them arguing or anything. Maybe Marine did since they share a wall."

"Hopefully not. I prefer my residents not having any complaints," he said as he took a deep inhale of the blanket. He grimaced. "Maybe she could have thrown out some words of wisdom for them though, I know her and Monte have been together a long while. Would have saved me having to clean up this mess," he turned to look back inside, "god knows if I'll be able to save the couch."

"You could just take it out of their deposit," I suggested, shrugging my shoulders. I was really only half interested in the conversation. I wouldn't want him to take money from a struggling couple, but I didn't know what else to say. My eyes kept darting around back to the book, like an awful poker tell.

"Yeaaah I guess I could. Hate to put the blame on the couple that lived here, they did try at least. You should see the messes some people leave. People steal the damn outlet covers," he looked surprised by his own curse and looked at me, "Sorry."

"No worries," I said.

"Thanks. Anyway, guess I can't stick this thing with the next resident. Guess I'll have to replace it, or at least get some pro in here to get it right. I don't even remember how we got these damn couches in here..." he trailed off. He turned to me again, "Well, back to it. Have a good one."

"You too, don't work too hard," I replied, adding a small nod bye.

I sat waiting for something else to happen. I listened hard at the balcony to see if he would come back out, but heard nothing. Nothing from the other balconies either. I hit the button on my phone to see what time it was, but it wasn't much of a help, as I didn't think to check the starting time of the "break". I considered going inside, my skin already feeling a good sear from the sun, but I was worried that whatever was happening would stop.

Later, I would realize how much I desired for this mystery to continue, I didn't want this odd sensation to end. I had no idea if what was happening was real anymore. It felt real, the daydream seemed so vivid. Like a dream you don't want to wake up from. It wasn't a good dream, but not bad either. Just interesting and I wanted to explore it more. Seeing the mountain, the machines filtering air, it was something that I had never created in my imagination, which gave me more of a reason to believe that this experience was truly happening.

That was fifteen minutes exactly; I hope that you are back to a comfortable position. My focus snapped back and my fingers ruffled pages until I found where I had left off. *The next thing to discuss is something simple that we must get out of the way, as it will help you accept the reality of the situation.*

"About how you are talking to me?" I cut in.

Yes, so you won't linger on the question anymore. Please realize the importance of how this happens and do not share the matter of how this is done with anyone else. At best, they will think you are crazy. That being said, we know that you won't.

The thought finished, seemingly waiting for me to catch up on my writing. Maybe he knew he had conveyed a lot for my scribbling hand, or maybe for a reply from me. I tried to think of a question, but I had far too many. Questions about who he was flooded my mind. I had wishes for more of the daydreams, questions about my own life in the future. Thankfully, my great-great-grandson interrupted my trailing mind.

Before you fell unconscious, a glint of light hit your eye. I can only imagine it being incredibly bright. In fact, had you not been knocked unconscious and forced to close your eyes, you may have been blinded for a good period of time. The light was sent by me and the scientists here in the distant future. In the simplest of terms, as it is over my head, by using a perfectly developed atmosphere, they can amplify pulses of light to such a level that it far exceeds the speed of light. Past the speed of light, the beam can travel backwards in time. Once the light is fast enough, they can manipulate the speed to narrow in on how much energy is needed to get to one time in particular.

Separate experiments had been done with strobing the light. Using light at an imperceptible high speed, they are able fire certain brain synapses in a desired order to trigger a person to have thoughts chosen by the sender. However, it was very experimental, as brains are very unique. Experiments with this required numerous scans, monitoring, and brain surgery to get the information required to see what synapses needed to be fired to make a simple thought. As you will eventually pass away, your brain was able to be thoroughly studied posthumously in our time that a living subject couldn't have done.

By utilizing these techniques, the scientists here sent a rapid flash of light from the future that triggers your brain to think in the ways that we had predetermined. The thoughts you are having now are all still effects of the earlier flash. I'll pause for you to catch up on writing.

I looked over the explanation with bewilderment after filling out a page and a half in my frantic penmanship, the side of my hand black from smeared ink. It seemed and still seems impossible, yet I'll never know how far science is able to advance in the years that follow me. This response at least slightly calmed my yearning for answers. I flipped the page I had just written over back and forth, thinking of what to ask next.

"You just said that I'm still being affected by the 'earlier flash', then how are you replying to me?" I said, hardly moving my lips.

I am not directly replying. I can't see or hear you. That is why your notes are so important, you are currently writing the script that I presented to the scientists, who then turned it into the premade flash of light. I won't be able to reply to anything you don't write down.

This was a strange idea, that I would be replying to myself. Though this certainly wasn't the strangest part of what had been happening. I thought I would see if that fact was accurate. I put my pen to the page.

"Oh, hello again Marine!" I lied both out loud and thought hard, in case the voice was actually listening in. At the same time, I wrote down, 'A large bird is landing on the balcony now, shoo it away', with a ?- in front of it. Even though I knew the thoughts were my great-great-grandson at that point, I didn't want to change my notation style from ?- to anything more complicated.

A large bird is landing on the balcony now, shoo it away, my mind thought on its own a moment later. It seemed like proof enough.

"I did," both lying and writing again, "but I have to know. If you are sending me the words I am writing down now, then am I just talking to myself?" The reply was something I've come to accept over the following years to this point, that or I created the whole conversation in my head.

I can only imagine this conversation being a slip of the mind that caused me to change my focus for my whole writing career.

In your day, it is common to think of time linearly, but it is more simultaneous. I have read the lines you wrote for me and sent you more accurate information, as what you wrote needed a bit of correcting. You are recording my messages in the past while I rewrote and sent what you are thinking in the future. I certainly had my doubts, and still do. It takes a lot of effort for me to believe that whatever I write now will happen someday, like it is all set-in stone or something. I can only assume that this is how time works, or else receiving a message from the future could change the future entirely. It seems we have free will to make our choices and our future, but I guess the future already knows every choice we will make.

It will take time for you to consider what has happened today, and even more to write your poetry, but using nature as your outlet will help the words come easier to you.

"Why can't you just tell me the poems to write?" I asked the paper. It would have saved me a lot of time, drafting and revising was something I always put off.

Because you will develop your poems over time and periodically release your work over multiple years. It will help the exponential strength of the future environmental movement that many more will join into. It will be hard, but you can and will get your poetry written, as it has already happened. Just changing a few minds is all it takes over the years. I paused for a moment, as the thoughts seemed to pause as well. Even though this was supposedly a distant relative, hearing about the ways I would help change the world only stressed me out. Looking back on these notes always felt like a parent promising that "You will succeed no matter what!" which puts all the more pressure on creating something substantial.

"If you can't tell me about the poems that I will write," I continued, "then what else can tell me?"

I can tell you that you will have trouble with love, as many do. You are very comfortable with being single, and being single suits you well, but just keep your mind open and don't renounce love, even if you have had difficulties with it in the past. I never had the chance to meet anyone further up our family tree than my grandparents, so I am only giving you the advice you suggested to yourself.

Being able to write about others in an open and meaningful way is what makes romantic poetry so sincere. If you knew who you were destined to be with, interactions with anyone else would be all a facade.

You aren't to pay this note too much mind, just that you should keep your options opened over the years.

I thought for a moment after that. Who is this voice telling me to focus on love and not these supposed upcoming natural disasters? This statement on my relationships was also true, but left an annoying, pissed off, sinking feeling in my gut. Like when a close friend lectures you over a mistake you made. As he mentioned, I had a few relationships in the past, some for long periods of time that made me realize that being more casual with dating was much less taxing. That and I always preferred to live on my own.

My great-great-grandson didn't share much more information with me about his experience with his ancestors. I suppose it was for a good reason. If I knew exactly who I would marry, I'd probably become obsessed with making that a reality. Honestly, I would most likely come off crazy. What he did share was more advice. He told me that I should try to find someone that challenged me in my creativity in a healthy way, and that I should get out of the house and travel more. To even move around the United States and see if anywhere else felt like home.

I'm glad I took the advice, even if I was hard-headed for a while. Knowing my supposed future made dating tricky. I was very reluctant to ever label myself in a relationship, purely out of spite. Thankfully I got over myself and took the advice only after deciding that it's okay to allow myself to get closer to others. Afterall, most others do. It was the best advice I had ever taken, as I am now happily married to a person that inspires me every day. Below is a poem I wrote after a few dates, when my feelings began to blossom:

WAKING UP

I step out onto the balcony, joining you in
the morning sun.
The birds seem to rise with you.
We hadn't spent a night together,
and this was the same but different,
you stayed
but with me on the couch.

We got a little drunk for the first time in a
while.
I'm happy to see you up early and at least hiding any headaches.
You already watered the plant boxes,
saving me the time from my daily chores.
Wouldn't mind you being around to do it
more often.

You start to fill a larger pot with soil from
a bag in the closet,
a pot I told you about last night,
a destination for the lilacs that need to be
transplanted.
I thank you for your help as I move the flowers to their new home.
You smile and ask if we can do it together.
Our fingers brush between the roots.

CHAPTER FOUR

PLOT

———

It's been a bit since I visited you.
The flowers I laid last week still have a
blush of color.

I've been doing better about stopping by,
but it is still hard to build up the strength,

or maybe the energy.

You never leave my mind.

I wonder if forgetting about you would help,
but I think I'm still trying to finish works
you saw me start.
Looking down at your roped off foot of land

MAKES ME WONDER IF YOUR ASHES HAVE BECOME
PART OF THE GARDEN AROUND YOU.

I THINK IT HAS.

THE FLOWERS SEEM TO GROW MORE VIBRANT HERE.
I STOOP DOWN AND PULL OUT THE FEW SPROUTING
CLOVER.

My father was an incredible man that helped raise me; something that I took for granted for most of my life. He had health problems for years, but it took a while until anything was considered terminal. When my mom started talking about how life would be different without him, about life insurance and the time we had together as a family even before he passed, I knew things were getting more serious. I was jaded to this fact, but when my great-great-grandson told me about part of my future work being inspired by a passed family member, I could make the assumption of who it would be.

The days leading up to his passing were a bit unexpected. In the last two weeks his health deteriorated quickly even though he had been sick for a long while. I couldn't help but vent at his bedside about how my brothers had done more than me; having started families, careers, all while I was still alone and working hourly. Not that I wasn't proud of them, just that I wanted him to see me in the same place as them. Maybe it was just my jealousy, my selfishness, my way to cope.

It was about three months after I had heard the voices in my head describe the vague loss of a family member that my dad passed. It was another handful of months before I felt up to writing again. Writer's block hit me like a steamroller. It was hard to find the words to try and summarize losing a loved one, as none of my words could live up to that weight. I would get drunk, depressed, and tell my inebriated self that "Tomorrow, I will get back to writing."

Always tomorrow.

Writing, and everything else, became a matter of tomorrow. I would set deadlines for everything; schooling, exercise, getting better jobs. If I knew my timeframe I could know when and where to put my effort. By the end of the year I would have my book done, a new car, a real "adult" job, have ran a marathon, get my mental health in order, an endless list.

Then, I would just watch the deadlines crept up. Knowing that, if heaven is a real thing, then my dad is looking down at me making excuses. Maybe I would have gotten more done if I was more confident that he was really up there. Who knows?

Everything happening around me felt like it turned me into a procrastinator, even though I had never been one growing up. Time seemed to crawl everyday, trudging through sand. It felt like there was always time because it never felt like anything would end. Then, a second late, another month on the calendar would scroll by.

It is still hard for me to accept that this voice in my head could have predicted something like my father passing, as it is a safe assumption that everyone's fathers pass away at some point. It was surreal to spend time with him, knowing that at some point he would pass. Maybe it was a bit of a curse to learn this, since whenever I was with him after hearing my great-great-grandson I had the thought of my dad's passing looming in the back of my head. Even more so than it already had been. Or was it the doctor's assessment? I would be enjoying my time with him, maybe playing a card game or getting dinner, and his stifled coughs would snap my attention to a future loss.

His passing put a strange weight on me. It had been such a long time since I had lived with him that he was somewhat removed from my life. That and I didn't talk to him as often as I should've. My daily life went back to normal after the funeral. My daily routine was unchanged. Some days I wouldn't think of him, whatever I did during the day just didn't bring him to mind. Not that I didn't love him, just that a day of work and cooking dinner and talking to friends and drinking some wine and paying bills can fill the mind. Other days I would be at the store and tear up in the aisles listening to a podcast we used to bond over. I would try and hide my face in the frozen food bunkers.

He was out of state when he was taken to the hospital, too sick to make it home and no one was sure how much time he had. All the family flew down to spend the vague amount of time we had left with him. He could have recovered enough to make it home. To get out of a strange city and be closer to our extended family members, but he faded quickly and we didn't know if it was possible. It was for the best that our direct family flew down to be with him. He passed while we were by his side about a week and a half later. Being overwhelmed by extended family sharing their condolences, while well-intentioned, sounded sickening.

The time I spent with him was something surreal. He had a breathing tube in for the two days that he was responsive. He would write notes on his end and I would try to make small talk the best I could. That is what made up the time we spent together, hours of it. That and fetching nurses to help him relieve himself. He would motion for me to leave the room, and I would. I couldn't bear to see the shame in his face.

The days following, he was put into a post medically induced sleep. I changed to sitting quietly. The silences were broken by my sniffling, speaking under my breath, snot banding my lips.

Every once in a while he would open his eyes. I couldn't tell if he knew where he was, but when he would look at me, his eyes would smile and give me a wink. Then close again. I don't know if he did this knowingly.

That week and a half was one of the few times of my life that I ran out of words. Watching television in the hospital room, the waiting room, the eventual hospice room, in my hotel room, and any other video on my phone were the only things that drew my mind's attention. It felt as if the week and a half was removed from the rest of time.

It wasn't until my family's long layover home, one family member less, that I was able to crack my notebook before a long writing hiatus:

A LONG, SHORT RIDE

Attention passengers, the 9:30 Rail will be departing shortly

I flip through pages in my notebook
trying to find words
inspiration
to use on the ride home.
Yet, my mind can't focus.
Eyes dart between paper and phone.
A family is leaving together,
smaller than when we arrived,
each feeling alone.

I gathered my things and walked with
my family onto the mag-train heading
cross-country. Home.

Doors will be closing shortly. We estimate a
trip of about two hours.

In a flash the towering city
the bright lights
reflective steel
cut to rolling sand hills.
Plots yet to be developed.
Occasional sections of roped off trees
large areas of land unfit for building.
The wind was whipping their leaves.
The speed of the passing train whipped back.

We sat in silence.
The train moved silently as well.
The sound slipping through brother's
headphones
was the loudest thing I could hear.

"Just a half hour left," the speakers cracked
"You'll all be home soon."

CHAPTER FIVE

S omeone else should be stepping out onto their balcony.

I looked up to see no one, which confused me.

Then, a moment later, I jumped in my seat as the balcony door to my right slid open partially. I watched as the door seemed to catch part of the way and the opener had to put some upward force to get the door to open about half of the way. A tired looking woman worked her way around the glass pane. She had a messy bun on the top of her head and was wearing a grey and white buffalo check robe over top of a black tank top and jeans. Upon getting through the door, her hands dove into her robe's pockets. The left came out empty and the right came out with a vape the size of a pack of gum. She stepped forward, leaned her forearms on the steel railings, and took a long drag from the plastic tip.

After a moment, a young boy, maybe six or seven, followed the woman onto the balcony, hands in his pockets. He looked at his mother for a brief second, looked at me, and then shifted his stare through the bars of the railing, watching the cars drive below. The robed woman took another puff and as she exhaled. She turned to me. Her eyes told me that me being there had just registered.

"Sorry, didn't realize anyone was out here," she said as she crossed her arms.

"Oh, don't worry about it," I replied with a bit of a smile. By this point I was a bit calmer than I was earlier in the day.

An awkward moment hung in the air as this woman I didn't know continued to rock in place. I sat, staring into space, still thinking over how strange this day had been, unsure if anything was real. I still question it. At some point the woman spoke up again.

"We just moved in from across town, from over on Dodge. I'm Jennifer and this is James," the woman said. She tousled his hair, "Say hi James, be polite."

"Hi," he said without moving his head.

"Hello James, nice to meet you. I'm Lynn. Are you having a good day?" I asked. Jennifer did a quiet sigh, one that carried some recent exasperation. She patted her son on the head lightly and resumed her stoic pose.

"It has been a bit of a... challenge getting James to look forward to his new school, he's gonna finish up his quarter and then transfer closer to here," she said. James continued staring off the balcony. I could notice that he was sad, even from this distance.

"Awww I'm sorry to hear about that James. I'm sure you will find plenty of friends at your new school, and I'm sure you can always see your old friends too," I reassured. He seemed to exhale a bit harder. "If you need one to get you started, I can be your friend too."

He looked up with a spark of disbelief in his eyes, mouth agape in disbelief. I smiled the friendliest smile I could muster. I've never been the best with kids but they always seemed to take a liking to me. My overacted smiles have yet to make any kids cry at least.

"What do you like to do James? Do you like video games?" I asked, to which he nodded slowly, almost cautiously. "Me too, I used to play them a lot more when I had the time, do you have a favorite?" To this he didn't reply.

"He's always playing that cartoony-block building one," his mother replied on his behalf.

"Ahh, I know the one, I play it too." To this his opened mouth turned into an opened grin. Jennifer gave a bit of a smile looking at him. She exhaled more smoke from pursed lips.

"So Lynn, if you don't mind me asking, what do you do for work? I'm a nurse at Children's down the way," Jennifer said.

"Well, I'm actually kind of part self-employed right now. I've been writing for a while now, like poetry and some stories. I do that and work weekends just down there," I said as I pointed to the supermarket down the block, "I'm thinking about applying to some places for a more stable job. But, I'm not sure about that anymore, this morning I've been," I hesitated a moment. I looked down and realized I still had the notepad in my lap and I almost instinctively wanted to hide it, but with the two looking at me I decided to play it more relaxed than throwing the note-book aside. "I don't know, thinking about a lot of things I guess."

"Oh that's interesting! James here actually had a haiku published in a book full of the best poems written by all the students at his school last year. It was something about our cat, do you remember it off the top of your head?" she said, patting James on the back. She motioned him in my direction. He thought for a moment, and again, he silently shook his head.

"That's okay, poems can be hard to remember," I reassured him with a nod, "I'm sure it's great and would love to hear it some time. I really like writing about animals too, and nature."

"Ya hear that James? You two like the same things! You should share a poem with us if ya have one!" Jennifer said excitedly. She seemed to be getting more interested in having someone cheer her son up.

"Well, honestly, I write some things that can be a little inappropriate for kids," I warned. To this, they both seemed deflated. "But, I could try and think of a haiku really quick for you James, if you want" an idea to which the two seemed to light up over. I nodded and thought for a few moments and scribbled this down in the margins of the paper still in my lap.

To James
    New Friendships

Clouds grin, leave curled smiles
Cats cry to make a new friend
From plants, trees, to me

I read it out loud for the mother and son and the two smiled

"Thank you for writing that, it was very sweet, say thank you to your new friend James," Jennifer said, patting James's back, motioning him to speak up.

"Thank you," he said, quietly but with a genuine smile.

"Oh no problem, it's always fun to share a hobby," I said. I wasn't sure how to fill the space.

"I can definitely tell you like writing about nature," Jennifer said with a chuckle almost like a children's television host in that way that parents tend to do when seeing if their children have learned anything, "Well, James and I need to go get some food in our systems, it was great to meet you Lynn. Say 'bye' James," Jennifer said warmly.

"Bye Lynn," the son said with a childish wave and smile.

"See ya around, 'nd welcome to the building," I said, waving back.

I sat a moment longer, still smiling as their door closed and my hand fell to my lap. I sat in the white noise of the city; my mind blank for the first time all day. The weather was beautiful. I felt comfortable, warm.

CHAPTER SIX

I sat for a few minutes until a driver a few blocks away laid on their horn. I looked in the direction of the sound, continued my steady breathing, turned to my notebook, and wrote down that I had finished my chat with my new neighbors after about twenty minutes. I sat patiently for a response. Maybe I had overestimated the twenty minutes. Looking back on it, the moment of silence I sat in was the most relaxing moment I had that day. I took another deep breath and felt my shoulders drop an inch as I exhaled. I could feel the knot in my shoulder forming from how tense I had been the whole day. I realized I was starving and exhausted. Above all that, I was craving a cold beer. Still, I just sat there, waiting.

After a bit longer, the voice came back.

Welcome back yet again. We have more to discuss than just your family and future. This is about more than just yourself and our family tree.

The thoughts echoed through my brain and, reflexively, I began the process of notating again, turning to a new sheet of paper. My hand relished the opportunity to rest its death grip from the pen, so it begrudgingly returned to its former claw.

"Well, what do you need to tell me about?" I asked

Let me show you some of the ways that the future is different. It will be up to you to focus on creating your poems. I know it may be hard, as you tend to use the lens of nature. That's alright. Take your time. Don't strain over deadlines. It will happen over years. I'll tell you now, you will never get the level of success you want deep down. Wanting to create for fame isn't a bad thing, everyone does it, but creating it for yourself is far more important.

Looking back on this, I still can't disagree. Yet, it's still hard to accept. I can't blame anyone that tries to create something looking for recognition. Thousands of people hope to get famous daily for their music, acting, art. Everyone wants praise. Yet, coming to terms with the fact that I want my work to be acknowledged is still something I have trouble coming to terms with.

My senses were stolen away from me yet again. I saw technology that I can only speculate on how it works or what it does. My eyes saw sights of what looked like futuristic news yet to break and movies that had never been made. My senses were filled with artificial nature. I can only dream of seeing where the future will lead us.

My great-great-grandson told me about many things, leaving me little time to interject. Little time to ask any questions. Hardly enough time to write down every detail, like trying to fill a journal about your last night's dream as it fades. I did my best to determine which parts were important and I tried to emphasize them in my notes.

I took my notes, my memories, and did my best to create poems over the coming weeks, months, and years. The topics did change, leaving my family life and love life to seem like minor details in the grand scheme of things.

He told me about education:

PASSING PERIOD

Cameron the frog sat in the terrarium of
the elementary hallway.
Through fogged glass
she would watch the students pass
heading from elective to elective
class to class.
Kindergarteners walk in two rows
grasping a guiding rope between them.
Children with bright smiles,
beautifully blended skin tones,
laughing in multiple languages.
Some putting hushing fingers to their lips
some with gloves and trowels in tow
on their way outside to their class garden.

The snails clinging to the side of the tank
spy a sixth grade class stroll by.
They giggle and flirt while unsupervised
making their way to Human Growth
to learn about ongoing bodily changes.
After that class they will head to the lab
to practice their coding.

The creeping moss of the tank senses new
footsteps.
The philosophy and religion teacher makes
her way to her new room.

SHE FLIPS THROUGH HER AGENDA FOR TODAY:

EXCERPTS FROM RELIGIOUS TEXTS ABOUT HOW

WOMEN SHOULD BE TREATED.

SHE PLANS OF HAVING THE STUDENTS DISCUSS THE

TOPIC,

THE LAST FEW CLASSES HAVE GONE SMOOTHLY.

He told me about industry:

FROM THE DEPTHS

I WATCHED A DOCUMENTARY TODAY.

A FRIEND SHOWED ME AFTER I ASKED IF THEIR

HEATING BILLS HAVE BEEN CHEAPER.

IT STARTED IN A DARK, SUFFOCATING CREVICE OF

OCEAN.

INDUSTRIAL ALLOYS RISE FROM THE PITCH BLACK

WATER.

THE NARRATOR DISCUSSES FORCES HIGHER THAN

MY MIND CAN FATHOM,

METRICS AND CHARTS SHOW THE DRILL IN THE

DEPTHS

CLAWING EVER DEEPER.

SILVER SCALED FISH SWIM BY

THE CAMERA AS IT DIVES.

THE SCHOOL NUMBERS THIN,

FINS TURN TRANSLUCENT,

BONES TO RUBBER.

CAMERA LIGHTS SWIRL WITH BIOLUMINESCENCE.
THE PLUNGE CONTINUES
PAST CREATURES NEWLY DISCOVERED,
CRUSTACEANS LIVING IN IMPOSSIBLE CONDITIONS,
UNDER PRESSURES THAT WOULD CRUMPLE OLDER
TECHNOLOGY.
MASSIVE PIPES RUSH A LIQUID WITH INCREDIBLE
HEAT CAPACITY DOWN INTO THE EARTH.
THE EARTH HEATS THIS LIQUID TO INCREDIBLE
TEMPERATURES
BEFORE IT IS BROUGHT BACK TO THE SURFACE,
BACK PAST THE EYES OF FISH THAT SHIMMER
JUST UNDER THE TOP LAYER OF WATER,
AND INTO MACHINES,
HARNESSING HEAT INTO BATTERIES.

He told me about technology:

A NIGHT IN

IT'S BEEN A BIT SINCE I WENT ON A DATE.
I HAD RESERVATIONS ON MEETING SOMEONE FROM
AN APP
AS EVERY CONVERSATION SEEMED TO GO NOWHERE,
BUT THEY SEEMED NICE.
THEY TOLD ME ABOUT A PLACE THEY HAD ATE,
STEAK GRILLED AT YOUR TABLE.

At about seven,
I moved to my side room,
donned headband and gloves,
hit a button
on the back of my hand
and glass came down in front of my eyes.

A swirling circle on a black screen.

Candlelight fills the dark,
Lighting the room to a comfortable warmth.
My mind is there.
Warm bread under my nose,
forks clash,
wine wets my lips.
Immersion

You looked incredible compared to me.
I should have refitted myself.

We laugh while quoting a show we both love,
choking from laughter on red wine,
sweet on my mind's lips.

After dessert,
rich molten lava cake,
we agree to go on a walk afterwards,
prolonging our first date.

A flicker.

A PARK IN THE SNOW.
THE PALM OF MY RIGHT GLOVE HEATS
AS YOURS DOES AS WELL.
MY HEADBAND ORDERS MY BODY TO SHIVER.
PINE TICKLES MY OLFACTORY.

OUR LIPS WARM ONE ANOTHERS
MILES APART.

That hour went by in near silence. The sound of cars commuting home or to the few popular Omaha bars filled the air. The scribbling of my pen stopped intermittently as a mix of images entered my head from what could be the distant future. An outside viewer would have seen nothing out of the ordinary. Just a person writing intently.

CHAPTER SEVEN

My sore fingers rose to rub my straining eyes. I realized they had been straining from reading in the steadily decreasing light. I pulled my hand away and saw the now darker black ink that stained the side of my hand. Some dried in the creases of my fingers from the morning, some still with sheen on the side of my palm. The streetlights had flipped on and there were far less cars filling the streets. I arched my chest forward. My lower back cracked like breaking twigs from sitting on a patio chair all day. I could feel my sweaty clothes clinging to my back and thighs.

Looking down, a young couple was walking past, maybe in high school. They seemed happy, holding one another and jokingly pushing one another away when a playful insult was made at the other's expense. Across the street, a man was putting rideshare scooters into the back of his beaten-up old van, most likely on his way home to charge them. The van's engine was choking on oil as it idled, the sounds bounced up to my balcony.

I moved up toward the edge of the seat, feeling the fabric of my shorts peel off my legs. I stared at the notebook in my lap, pages like ribbons with sweat damage. I dropped my pen to the paper and tried to sooth my eyes with my fingers. My mind felt like a weight had been lifted off my brain. Yet, a different weight began to settle in and I looked at my note. The strange, uncertain weight of the task before me. This would be a long task, one that would take years. The rest of my life if my great-great-grandson was right. That is, if anything from that day was more than just a fever-dream.

Those images were the last thoughts that I received from him. I would never hear from him again or meet him during my lifetime. At least, at the point of writing this. Until writing this, the only person I ever mentioned this day to was my partner, and even then I withheld details. I realized when it happened, and still realize just how unbelievable this all was. So, I kept this to myself. As my day finally started to wind down, I had to do my best to get a grasp on the situation and handle it realistically.

I set my notebook and pen on the balcony table. As I slowly stood up, feeling the tension in my body build like a spring, I arched my stomach outward. I placed my hands on my lower back and rotated over each shoulder, making my spin rattle off like a gun. I stood back up and played an encore with my knuckles. I took a deep breath through my nose and tried to steady myself as my lightheadedness caused the world around me to swirl.

It wasn't until a moment later that the exhaustion rushed back. Focusing on a single topic for so long seemed to have drained me, even though I had been sitting on my butt all day. I could also feel my stomach starting to eat itself. I turned and gathered my things, feeling misplaced in a new world. Or the same world. I tucked my notebook up under my arms. I walked to my balcony door and opened it lazily, took a step inside, and as the door slid closed, I heard the tracks of the next door balcony open again.

I continued to slide my door shut, the day had proven too draining to want to play polite with my neighbors yet again, but my curiosity pulled my eyes through the glass door. As my door clicked into place, I could see James struggle to work his frame through the heavy door he could only get partially opened. In his hand was a small flower pot full of watered soil, a small sprout finding itself in a new home in the center of the pot. He stumbled a bit upon exiting the door, but after regaining his center he stepped forward and placed the pot in the corner of the balcony that still had a shred of sunlight. He stayed in a squat and rotated the plant until the leaves faced a direction that he seemed satisfied with. I couldn't make out the words, but I could hear James talking happily to the little sprout, no doubt making promises of daily baths and CO_2 filled conversations. His small left hand threw a finger over his left shoulder, blindly pointing at my door. I can only guess that he was telling his new child about meeting me.

Seeing James in this moment made my heart flutter, a feeling that I have chased in my writing ever since. Prior to that day I had always known that I wanted to make others enjoy my writing, but after this day I realized that even if my words could reach just a couple individuals, someday they could help change the minds of others as well. But it still scares me, I can never be sure on what influence I will have, no matter what I hope happens. Someone can only do so much, and I don't even know what that "so much" entails. Just sharing my thoughts, I suppose. Looking back on my younger self at that time, I was already concerned that the world around me was bleak, but I've learned that it is never too late to start rectifying.

I let out a breath, smiling to myself as I did so, and slowly closed the blinds behind me out to the balcony. My stomach told me I was ready for food, my body; a shower, and my mind; bed.

I gathered these former poems from over the years, as well as others, and put them into a short collection. I made some revisions over time as well as where I saw fit.

PART TWO
BRONZE-WINGED BUTTERFLY

GREEN ENERGY

Electric cables run the trunk
and branches of the oak tree,
laying flush against the wood,
following grooves of the tree's bark.
Color a close match to the tree's brown.
Cables split off
at different forks and branches,
stretching to arms' ends
and connect small solar panels
that rest upon each leaf.
The artificial tree pumps photosynthesis
to its roots and batteries.

SWEAT AND WATER

The heat bares down on you,
as you like it to do,
while in our garden pruning stray stems.
I love to watch and hear your quite giggles
about the aesthetic choices I suggest.
For fun I tell you to lop off whatever flower looks the best.
It's been an hour.
After doing my own,
I apply more sunscreen to the back of your neck, already pink.
Bending over you with a towel,
I dab your sweat
and count how many flowers you have left.
Just a small row.
Still bent, I pick up your water bottle
and sprinkle it onto the artificial flowers.
You giggle again.

ZOO

I've been spending a lot of time at the zoo lately.
It hasn't been cheap after they moved it underground.
But, like any newer place looking for land,
there is more room down there.
There is actually space to watch the elephants
happily race under their radiant sunlight panels.
It still smells like any ol' zoo.
A couple times a month they even have a "Rain Day"
where sprinklers mist down on awestruck observers.
The petting zoo is always a sight to see.
Children cooing at chickens and cows
since they haven't seen them before.
Like aliens from another planet.

DIRTY TO STALE

The air is always stale.
Pure, but stale.
Clouds of smog and carbon
are filtered through
the tall, steel towers on the mountain ridge.
Massive tunnels on V-shaped legs,
filthy on one side from the thick air,
like a black moss on a metal trunk.
There are few other trunks scattered around.
A once thick forest traded for a grey-brown rock face.
Lasers remove the C of CO_2.
I've heard that you can hear the popping when they work overtime.
It's efficient,
"Saves space," they tell us,
"They make plenty of air."

BRONZE-WINGED BUTTERFLY

Photovoltaic cells stretch thin
over wings that pound,
lifting the metal butterfly
off the ground
gentle and slow.
Its glass abdomen half-full of eggs
waivers in its weight.
Sensors in its compound eyes spy
a patch of green,
now often few and far between.
The butterfly touches down
and softly lays the eggs on a waiting leaf that,
by the butterfly's determination,
leaves a bit less than an 87% chance at survival.
Far above the release threshold.
Even further above the rate if a natural butterfly picks the location.
The Natural Beauty Initiative aims to reestablish feigning species
while still looking visually appealing.

WAKING UP

I step out onto the balcony, joining you in the morning sun.
The birds seem to rise with you.
We hadn't spent a night together,
and this was the same but different,
you stayed
but with me on the couch.

We got a little drunk for the first time in a while.
I'm happy to see you up early and at least hiding any headaches.
You already watered the plant boxes,
saving me the time from my daily chores.
Wouldn't mind you being around to do it more often.
You start to fill a larger pot with soil from a bag in the closet,
a pot I told you about last night,
a destination for the lilacs that need to be transplanted.
I thank you for your help as I move the flowers to their new home.
You smile and ask if we can do it together.
Our fingers brush between the roots.

PLOT

It's been a bit since I visited you.
The flowers I laid last week still have a blush of color.

I've been doing better about stopping by,
but it is still hard to build up the strength,

or maybe the energy.

You never leave my mind.

I wonder if forgetting about you would help,
but I think I'm still trying to finish works you saw me start.
Looking down at your roped off foot of land
makes me wonder if your ashes have become
part of the garden around you.

I think it has.

The flowers seem to grow more vibrant here.
I stoop down and pull out the few sprouting clover.

A LONG, SHORT RIDE

Attention passengers, the 9:30 Rail will be departing shortly

I flip through pages in my notebook
trying to find words
inspiration
to use on the ride home.
Yet, my mind can't focus.
Eyes dart between paper and phone.
A family is leaving together,
smaller than when we arrived,
each feeling alone.

I gathered my things and walked with my family onto
the mag-train heading cross-country. Home.

Doors will be closing shortly. We estimate a trip of about two hours.

In a flash the towering city
the bright lights
reflective steel
cut to rolling sand hills.
Plots yet to be developed.
Occasional sections of roped off trees
large areas of land unfit for building.
The wind was whipping their leaves.
The speed of the passing train whipped back.

We sat in silence.
The train moved silently as well.
The sound slipping through brother's headphones
was the loudest thing I could hear.

The images of you still haven't left my mind.
Both the happy and sad.
I stare at my translucent reflection in the window,
watching the sheen of unwiped tears on its cheek.

"Just a half hour left," the speakers cracked
"You'll all be home soon."

TO JAMES
NEW FRIENDSHIPS

Clouds grin, leave curled smiles
Cats cry to make a new friend
From plants, trees, to me

TO LYNN
WHEN I SEE YOU AGAIN

In my life I've grown
You helped me smile like the sun
I hope you shine too

DANCING WATER

Children's laughs bounce from the wet walls,
From street to street,
as rain falls straight down,
threading towering buildings.
Humidity levels never seem to drop.
Water that falls evaporates faster than in the past.
It's common for the warm rain
to tap on windows and doors
to call the kids out to play
on warm spring/summer/winter/fall days.

PASSING PERIOD

Cameron the frog sat in the terrarium of the elementary hallway.
Through fogged glass
she would watch the students pass
heading from elective to elective
class to class.
Kindergarteners walk in two rows
grasping a guiding rope between them.
Children with bright smiles,
beautifully blended skin tones,
laughing in multiple languages.
Some putting hushing fingers to their lips
some with gloves and trowels in tow
on their way outside to their class garden.

The snails clinging to the side of the tank
spy a sixth grade class stroll by.
They giggle and flirt while unsupervised
making their way to Human Growth
to learn about ongoing bodily changes.
After that class they will head to the lab
to practice their coding.

The creeping moss of the tank senses new footsteps.
The philosophy and religion teacher makes her way to her new room.
She flips through her agenda for today:
excerpts from religious texts about how women should be treated.
She plans of having the students discuss the topic,
the last few classes have gone smoothly.

GREEN AND POPULAR

Nationally mandated arboretums are to be planted state to state.
Obviously for historical purposes at this point.
It will make a nice day trip to take the children
to see trees, climb, get splinters,
scrapping knees for the first time.
I liked the new president's policies on the environment,
that's why I voted for them.
A new president each year only lets them get their best ideas in place,
and with a majority vote,
it makes a popularity contest the race.

A NIGHT IN

It's been a bit since I went on a date.
I had reservations on meeting someone from an app
as every conversation seemed to go nowhere,
but they seemed nice.
They told me about a place they had ate,
Steak grilled at your table.

At about seven,
I moved to my side room,
donned headband and gloves,
hit a button
on the back of my hand
and glass came down in front of my eyes.

A swirling circle on a black screen.

Candlelight fills the dark,
Lighting the room to a comfortable warmth.
My mind is there.
Warm bread under my nose,
forks clash,
wine wets my lips.
Immersion

You looked incredible compared to me.
I should have refitted myself.

We laugh while quoting a show we both love,
choking from laughter on red wine,
sweet on my mind's lips.

After dessert,
rich molten lava cake,
we agree to go on a walk afterwards,
prolonging our first date.

A flicker.

A park in the snow.
The palm of my right glove heats
as yours does as well.
My headband orders my body to shiver.
Pine tickles my olfactory.

Our lips warm one anothers
miles apart.

A FALL

An angel lent me her wings
for a moment
so I could look down and see you
through the tops of the trees you walk beneath.
With each flutter
I drop a feather
near you, tickling you, making you smile.
I beat the wings
to make a fragile, white rain
so the light in your eyes wouldn't disappear.
You always loved birds,
but they always stayed far north of the cities.
With a final thrust, the wings went bare,
blood dropped from the holes of quills not there.
And I fell
to the trees above you,
flapping the bald, skin wings on my back
as you walked away,
still trying to make you smile.

CRUEL TIDES

Inspired by "Acorn Duly Crushed" by Heather Christle

Dear filthy ocean.
Dear polluted water.
What am I supposed to do?
Are you too far gone?
There is plenty of water.
We need to ship goods.
Thin iron beams branch you,
leaving you striped in metal.
Massive platforms race their length,
storage containers in tow.
Dear mood-swinging
endless ocean.
Too many crustaceans
and unnatural creatures
live in your dark crevices.
They are horrible,

nightmares.
Monsters that keep me up at night.
Dear fickle, sweet ocean.
You carry surfers and boats,
cars and houses
out with your tide.
We build higher.
The moon steers your waves.
Don't you make
your own choices?
Tell me about
the millions of fish
having sex,
being born,
and eating other fish.
Dear freezing bounty.
How can I see
every part of you?
I can't afford
to fly across your
breadth.

ABOUT THE AUTHOR

Luke R. Gregerson developed a bond with nature poetry and fantastical imagery while attending Nebraska Wesleyan University as both an English and music major. He also attended the Juniper Institute for Young Writers, where he broadened his knowledge of different poetry forms. After graduating, he moved to Japan to teach English, as well as attain his master's in Library and Information Sciences.

CPSIA information can be obtained
at www.ICGtesting.com
Printed in the USA
LVHW041641180122
708821LV00007B/534

9 781665 714747